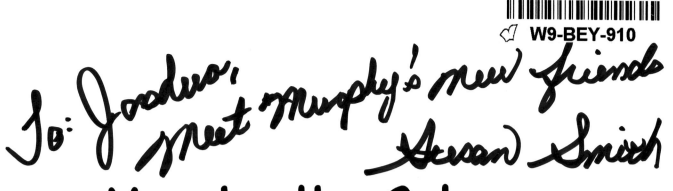

To: Joshua, meet Murphy's new friends
Susan Smith

Murphy the Cat
And His
New Friends

by
Susan Smith

Illustrated by
Don Higgins

Murphy had just moved into his big yellow house in his new neighborhood.

He had met one new friend, the lady next door in the grey house with the black shutters and red door.

One day Murphy decided to explore his new neighborhood.

He left his house and walked down the street.

He wondered how many more new friends he would meet.

Will he meet one, two, three, or four new friends?

Where could he go to meet new friends?

The woods behind the tall houses seemed to be a good place to start.

He saw a squirrel climbing up a tree, birds working very hard to build their nests and a small mouse sitting on a rock enjoying the bright warm spring sun.

His fur was auburn and he had big ears which were pink inside and a tail that looked like a worm.

The mouse ran, jumped and played with Murphy.

What fun Murphy thought.

The mouse told him his name was Benjamin.

Murphy had found another new friend. Now he as two friends in his new neighborhood.

Murphy told Benjamin about his big yellow house. He asked him where he lived.

Benjamin took him to a little hole in the ground.

"This is where I live," Benjamin said.

Murphy had never seen where a mouse lived before.

He thought; his house is soo small and mine is soo big.

Murphy could not fit inside Benjamin's house.

When he came to play they would have to play outside.

Murphy told Benjamin about his family and the tall men carrying the boxes when he moved into his new home.

He asked Benjamin if he had a family.

Benjamin said, "Yes."

"I have a mommy and a daddy, and a brother, and a sister."

"That's nice," Murphy said.

"I would like to meet them."

"Are they home," he asked?

"No," said Benjamin.

"They are all outside playing in the woods."

"Oh." said Murphy."

Murphy asked Benjamin if he would like to walk up the street.

Benjamin said "yes".

Murphy wanted to show him his big yellow house.

Murphy was so excited about his new friend.

He decided to take him to visit the Lady.

The two arrived at the Lady's house.

They walked right up the steps onto the deck and peeked in the big glass doors.

As always, the Lady was in the kitchen.

In just a few minutes she saw Murphy and his new friend.

Murphy and Benjamin were hungry and wanted a morning snack.

He told Benjamin to be on his best behavior.

Benjamin did his best to sit up on his back legs with his front feet right in front of him.

The Lady recognized Murphy.

She was happy to see him and his new friend.

She smiled at Benjamin and handed them a treat.

Murphy was very happy and did his best to purr
thanking the Lady for giving them a treat.

Murphy and Benjamin went on their way.

Murphy saw some children walking down the street.

He asked Benjamin where they were going?

Benjamin said he didn't know, but each day a big yellow bus picks them up and off they go.

It brings them home in the afternoon.

It was getting late.

It was almost
time for
supper.

Just as Murphy
and Benjamin were
saying good-bye
it started to rain.

Benjamin hurried
down the street
to his house.

Murphy went
home too.

When he got there his family wasn't home.

He could not get into his house and he was getting very wet.

Cats don't like to get wet.

He decided to return to the Lady's house.

Maybe she would let him in.

He went to the back door and scratched as loud as he could on the glass doors.

The Lady came to the door and let him in.

She dried him off and gave him some food.

Murphy felt much better.

After he ate he walked into the living room.

There was a fire in the fire place.

He curled up in front of it.

He was nice and warm.

The Lady walked in and saw that Murphy was dry and happy.

She decided to let him stay all night.

The next day Murphy went home.

He was happy to find
that his family had
returned.

Murphy stayed
home for a little
while, before he
decided to go
outside again,
walk down the
street, meet
Benjamin and
see if they could
meet any
more friends.

Murphy was excited.

Off he went with Benjamin.

It wasn't long before Benjamin stopped at the home of Pep the rabbit.

Pep's house was very different from other rabbits.
It was special.

He lived in
a rabbit hole
a little bigger
than Benjamin's
mouse hole.

His home was
built in a big
tree trunk.

It had a door shaped like a triangle and inside was Pep's rabbit hole.

Murphy and Benjamin met Pep just hopping out for his morning walk.

Benjamin introduced Murphy and Pep.

Now there were three friends. The Lady, Benjamin and Pep.

Murphy, Benjamin and Pep walked together in the woods behind the big houses.

Pep ran faster than Murphy and Benjamin.

The three friends ran deep into the woods.

There they discovered a small pond.
A family of ducks were swimming enjoying the spring day.

"We are the Mallard Family", said the mother duck. "We live here in this small pond. It is a special place hidden by all the tall trees."

Murphy, Benjamin and Pep visited for a while.
Then they went on their way.

They walked out of the woods, back into the neighborhood.

As they were just about to cross the street, Murphy saw another cat that looked just like him.

Murphy walked right up to meet her.

"Whats your name?" he asked.

"Ticksey", she replied.

"Oh that's a beautiful name for a little girl cat," he said.

"Where do you live?"

"Right over there in the tan house with the brown shutters" she said.

Her house was right across the street from Murphy's first best friend, the Lady.

Ticksey told Murphy that a very nice lady took care of her.

Murphy was happy
she had such a nice family.

I am very lucky thought Murphy as he said good-bye to his friends and went home to his big yellow house.

I have lots of new friends in my neighborhood.

They are Benjamin, Pep, The Mallard Family, and Ticksey.

But the most important one of all, was The Lady.